To Dragon and Zee —CZ

To all shy children with a tiger inside —MAM

Adobe Photoshop was used to prepare the full color art.

Published by Sourcebooks Jabberwocky, an imprint of Sourcebooks, Inc.
P.O. Box 4410, Naperville, Illinois 60567-4410
(630) 961-3900
Fax: (630) 961-2168
sourcebooks.com

Originally published as *A Tiger Called Thomas* in 1963 in the United States by Lothrop, Lee & Shepard.

Library of Congress Cataloging-in-Publication Data

Names: Zolotow, Charlotte, 1915-2013, author.
Title: A tiger called Tomás / Charlotte Zolotow.
Description: Naperville, Illinois : Sourcebooks Jabberwocky, 2017. | Summary:
   After moving, Tomás is reluctant to make new friends until he experiences
   a special night of trick-or-treating.
Identifiers: LCCN 2015039340 | (alk. paper)
Subjects: | CYAC: Moving, Household—Fiction. | Loneliness—Fiction. |
   Friendship—Fiction. | Halloween—Fiction.
Classification: LCC PZ7.Z77 Ti 2017 | DDC [E]—dc23 LC record available at https://lccn.loc.gov/2015039340

Source of Production: Leo Paper, Heshan City, Guangdong Province, China
Date of Production: April 2018
Run Number: 5012068

Printed and bound in China.
LEO 10 9 8 7 6 5 4 3 2 1

A Tiger
Called
Tomás

Charlotte Zolotow
Marta Álvarez Miguéns
—Afterword by Crescent Dragonwagon—

sourcebooks
jabberwocky

There once was a little boy named Tomás.

He was very nice.

But when he and his family moved to a new house on a new street, he took it into his head that the new people might not like him.

So he never left his stoop.

"Why don't you play with that little girl Marie?" his *mamá* asked him.

"Maybe she wouldn't like me," Tomás said.

"Of course she'd like you," his *mamá* said. "Why wouldn't she? *¿Por qué no?*"

But Tomás didn't answer.

"Why don't you visit the lady with the black cat down the street?" his *mamá* asked.

"They might not like me," Tomás said.

"Of course they'd like you. Why shouldn't they like you? *¿Por qué no?*" said his *mamá*.

But Tomás didn't go.

"That tall boy named Gerald looks lonely," his *mamá* said.

"I don't think he'd like me," said Tomás.

"Of course he'd like you," said Tomás's *mamá*. "Why shouldn't he like you? *¿Por qué no?* Everybody likes you."

But Tomás wouldn't leave his stoop.

He sat there and watched when Marie played hopscotch.

He sat there and watched the old woman's cat as it prowled through the grass and shrubs.

He sat there and watched when Gerald walked past the house, and he thought about how tall he was.

"Oh, Tomás," said his *mamá*. "Everyone will like you. Why don't you go play?"

But Tomás shook his head and just sat on the steps…watching.

The lady in the house across the street was always out in her yard, watering the plants, raking the leaves, sweeping the walk, picking her flowers.

And all the while, Tomás sat on his stoop and watched.

He watched the old man who came up the
street with his big black poodle three times a
day. The poodle always looked over its shoulder
at Tomás, and its tail stood up like a small palm
tree and wagged from side to side.

But Tomás just sat on his steps and
watched them pass.

He watched the sparrows and the grackles and
the blue jays in the trees. He watched the black cat
look up at the sparrows and grackles and blue jays.
But he never went off the stoop to play.

On Halloween, his *mamá* came home with a tiger costume for him.

"Try this on," she said. Tomás put on the orange-and-black-striped suit with its quilted tail.

He put on the mask with its long whiskers.

"How do I look?" he asked his *mamá.*

"Exactly like a *tigre,*" she said.

Tomás looked in the mirror, and his *mamá* was right.

"No one will know who I am when I go trick-or-treating," he said.

There was a large orange moon in the sky, and it was already getting dark when Tomás went out. The branches of the trees hardly showed, except where they laced across the moon.

He crossed the street to the house of the lady who was always outside. The chrysanthemums were still blooming in front of her house.

"Trick or treat!" Tomás called when she came to the door.

"Well, hello!" the lady said. She dropped a package of orange candies into his bag. "Happy Halloween."

"Thank you," answered the tiger.

"You're welcome, Tomás," the lady said, closing the door.

Under his mask, Tomás flushed.

"That's funny," he said to himself. "She called the tiger Tomás."

At the next house he rang the bell.

"Trick or treat!" he called.

Marie's mother opened the door. She had candy apples for the treat.

"Oh, thank you," the tiger said, for he especially liked candy apples.

"You're welcome," said Marie's mother. "Marie is a witch tonight. Maybe you'll pass her. But anyway, come play hopscotch here tomorrow, Tomás."

"Thank you," Tomás said again. But when the door closed, he reached up to feel his mask. It was still on, covering his whole face.

That's funny, he thought. *She knew who I was too.*

He passed a tall ghost going up to the house as he left.

He couldn't see the ghost's face, but there was something very familiar about this figure.

"Hi, Tomás," said the ghost. "Want to play horseshoes tomorrow? I got a new set."

"Sure," said Tomás. The ghost was Gerald. Tomás could tell by the height.

He went to the old man's house.

The black poodle threw back his head and barked wildly when he saw the tiger at the door. But when he sniffed at the tiger's feet and sniffed at the tiger's quilted tail, he suddenly put up his own palm-tree tail and wagged it hard.

"Trick or treat," the tiger said.

The old man had made big pumpkin cookies. "Fresh baked, Tomás," he said, winking as he dropped one in the bag. "Best thing for tigers," he added and winked again as he watched the tiger go down the steps.

He called the tiger Tomás too, thought Tomás.

Now he rang the bell at the house of the old lady and the black cat.

"Trick or treat!" he called.

"Come in, come in," the little old woman said. Her black cat looked curiously at the tiger, and the tiger reached out to stroke the cat's black, slippery fur.

"He loves that." The little old lady laughed. "Come play with him again, Tomás," she said. "He gets lonely."

"So do I," said Tomás.

She knew too, he thought to himself as he turned toward home.

The orange moon was a little higher in the sky. The sky was a little blacker than before. He couldn't see any of the branches against it now.

A group of ghosts and goblins was coming down the steps of the lady across the street. And a solitary but familiar-looking witch with her broom under her arm passed him. He looked at her curiously as he walked slowly toward the steps of his house. It was Marie.

"Hi, Tomás," called Marie.

Tomás walked upstairs to his own room. He looked in the mirror at the tiger. At the *tigre*. The *tigre* in the mirror looked back at him, whiskers and all.

"Have a good time?" asked his *mamá*.

"How did they know who I was?" Tomás asked.

"Did they?" said his *mamá*.

"Yes," Tomás said. "The mask didn't fool them a bit. And they all asked me to come back."

"I guess they all like you," his *mamá* said.

Tomás looked at her. Suddenly he felt wonderful… *maravilloso.*

"Oh, I like them too!" he said.

And when he took off the mask, he was smiling.

A Tiger Called Tomás... and a Writer Called Charlotte

Charlotte had once been a shy, lonely little girl. A little girl who—because her family moved a lot (from Norfolk, Virginia, to Detroit, Michigan, to Brookline, Massachusetts, and finally to New York City)—was the new girl, over and over, in school and in her neighborhood. A little girl who, because she wore big thick glasses and a large corrective back brace for almost two years, looked different, and, she thought, looked ugly. A little girl who was Jewish in neighborhoods that sometimes were not. A little girl who preferred quietly watching and listening to speaking, and who preferred engaging with the world through reading and writing to direct conversation.

"They might not like me," Tomás thinks of his new neighbors. In his feelings, in his self-doubt so strong it is almost certainty, Tomás is the shy, little girl Charlotte.

My mother wrote many picture books. *A Tiger Called Thomas* was first published in 1963, and then re-illustrated in 1988 and 2003. As her books were issued and reissued over time, many of those illustrators changed the skin color of the main characters from white to black, with Charlotte's hearty approval. The same evolution occurred with the third reissue of *A Tiger Called Thomas* in 2003, and the ever-unstated reason for Thomas's shyness and misgivings got another dimension when illustrator Diana Cain Bluthenthal made Thomas black.

And now in 2018 we come to Thomas's fourth incarnation, Tomás. Latino children are often bilingual, so I thought making Tomás Latino would add yet another layer to his universal story: showing that his isolation felt as much about language as it was about skin color.

I feel Charlotte would have approved of Tomás.

Tomás, that lonely little boy, takes courage from disguising his real self behind a tiger mask. Charlotte, once a lonely little girl, found solace in her quiet manner and her retreat into writing.

Yet just as his neighbors see through the mask to discover the real Tomás, Charlotte's very act of authorial hiding shows her to us clearly. In the end, just like Tomás, she stands revealed, and discovers how loved she, Charlotte Shapiro Zolotow, really was.

Charlotte Zolotow (1915–2013) wrote hundreds of stories, more than ninety of which were published, and two of which won Caldecott Honor Awards. She edited hundreds of other books in her tenure at Harper Brothers (now HarperCollins), where she eventually had her own imprint and became a vice-president in an office she kept full of houseplants. The mother of two children and the wife of show business biographer Maurice Zolotow, she mentored dozens of children's book authors, illustrators, and editors. You can find her at CharlotteZolotow.com, on Facebook at Charlotte Zolotow, and her Pinterest feed, which offers dozens of her pictures of her and illustrations of her books.

Crescent Dragonwagon is Charlotte Zolotow's daughter, literary executor, and the author of fifty published books in five genres. She leads "Fearless Writing" workshops all over the world and online. You can learn more about her at dragonwagon.com, and on Facebook at Crescent Dragonwagon's Writing, Cooking, & Workshops.